T0246958

STERLING CITY

STERLING CITY

STEPHEN GRAHAM JONES

OPEN ROAD

INTEGRATED MEDIA
NEW YORK

ISBN: 979-8-3372-0005-7

This edition published in 2024 by Open Road Integrated Media, Inc.
180 Maiden Lane
New York, NY 10038
www.openroadmedia.com

for Joe Luis Ferrer

STERLING CITY

1.

The night Zoe left, it rained fire. At least on the ten o'clock news. Lee watched it from his favorite chair and tilted his head over to better hear her out front, grinding the starter on her station wagon. He smiled then covered his mouth with his hand, like she could still catch him smiling. Next, because he always left the key in the ignition, she was at his truck. The clutch on it was gone, though; it would start, but unless you knew how to work the gas pedal, you couldn't keep it started. Zoe didn't know how to work the gas pedal. Lee smiled and nodded, and watched the news, only winced when he heard the cab door on his tractor close. Zoe couldn't even get it to turn over. Lee raised his beer, narrowed his eyes at the news.

The fire that was raining down was millions of miles away, in space. As near as anybody could tell, what had happened was that some moon around Mars was a lot more hollow than anybody would have guessed. All it took to pop the crust was one eight-pound probe. It had had a blunt nose, even. The pictures of it looked cartoonish to Lee, like the footage of the rounded-off A-bombs that had floated down onto Hiroshima and Nagasaki. Or maybe that had been in the movies.

Lee hitched his shoulders up in pain when he heard the starter on Zoe's station wagon grinding again.

He didn't think she would sleep out there, but it was March, warm enough, so who knew.

According to what she'd said from the doorway, anywhere would be better.

Lee used the remote control to change to the other news, try to catch the weather. It was still that moon, though, Phobos. Like that was all that mattered. How it was supposed to be an asteroid from way out there, not really even a moon at all. Over this news-caster's shoulder, the way they'd animated it made it look to Lee like a spore, like what he'd always imagined pollen looked like close up: powdery, round, pocked with craters. Only, now, after millions and billions of years, that biggest crater had opened, was breathing.

What the newsman said was, come May, when Earth started drifting into the debris field, there were going to be northern lights, and southern lights, and eastern and western lights. A once-in-a-lifetime meteor shower.

"But will it rain?" Lee said back to him, not really a question, and looked over the top of the set at the refrigerator.

Outside, there were no more sounds of Zoe.

Five minutes later, his beer drained, Lee guided himself up from the chair, cleared his throat, and pushed the storm door open. The idea was to call out to Zoe to turn the dome light off—didn't she *ever* want the station wagon to start again?

But then the dome light wasn't on.

At the edge of his field of vision, Lee could just see her. She was in her nightgown, running across the field through the stubble of wheat he needed to plow under sooner or later.

A quarter mile ahead of her, across the winter wheat and the low spot he usually saved for alfalfa, was the retired professor's house.

Lee was pretty sure the lights were still on there.

* * *

4

Doby woke him the next morning. Lee thought he was dreaming at first, that the deep roar in his head was because an eight-pound probe had touched down to the surface of the earth, punctured it, and now it was venting too, but then it was just his tractor out front. Doby was warming it up for the day. Unlike Zoe, he knew the angle to hold the choke so it would catch.

Lee rubbed his eyes with the heels of his hands and sat up from his chair.

What he told Doby when he finally made it outside was to pull the circle system over to the other pivot, to give the east side of the field a taste of water.

Doby eyeballed the fourteen joints of the circle system.

"Four wheels per joint," Lee said, leaning over to trail a line of spit down, rub it in with his boot.

It would take Doby most of the afternoon.

"Thought you wanted to . . . y'know, cut that stubble?" Doby said, shrugging. He was sixteen. His girlfriend, a redhead named Stace Collinworth, sat in the turnrows while he worked some afternoons, so she could talk to him, offer him drinks of her coke. Some of those afternoons, Lee had seen Zoe sitting with her, the two of them just talking. Through his windshield, it had been hard to tell one from the other.

Lee shrugged about the stubble Doby was talking about. The kid was right. They'd been talking about disking the wheat under for two weeks already, so he could list, then plant. But that was before last night, before Lee'd seen Zoe trying to run through that stubble. It couldn't have been easy.

"It'll wait," Lee said.

Two hours later, lunch for the rest of Sterling City, Lee stepped out of the barn, raised his welding mask, and focused in on the commotion the tractor had all of the sudden become. Doby had it gunned up like he was already pulling the—no, like

5

he was *racing*. Trying to get away from something. Except the tractor wasn't moving. It was in neutral. Just sitting there at the head of the circle system, diesel smoke billowing up in a thick column, the exhaust flap wide open, standing up on its hinge.

Lee shook his head, bit the thumb of his right glove to pull it off, and bared his teeth: Doby was trying to get his attention. Trying to call Lee out there, instead of walking in himself to ask whatever the question was: a jammed cotter pin, a broke chain, the pin on the jack jammed into the shaft again.

He'd walk out there all right.

After last night, it would feel good even, to make Doby cower in an open field. Halfway there, though, he slowed, stopped, turned his head away from the tractor, suddenly sure what Doby had found: Zoe, stumbled into the 440 extension cord at the pivot, cooked to a crisp.

Lee started breathing deep, shaking his head no, and then like a sign, like an omen, fell into some of Zoe's tracks. Doby hadn't found her. Her tracks were right there, two-to-a-furrow, meaning she'd had to step over each row individually. They didn't lead to the pivot, were parallel with the circle system.

Lee hated her anyway, even if she wasn't dead.

When Doby finally saw him, he throttled the tractor back, then, instead of stepping down, climbed out onto the hood, his hat in his hand.

Lee looked in the direction of the professor's house, shook his head in disgust for anybody watching through binoculars. When he was close enough that Doby could see him, he made the cut-off sign, for him to kill the tractor.

In the silence it left, he could almost hear Doby breathing.

"Kid," he said, "you better—" but then never finished.

Doby wasn't just breathing hard. He was crying, about to wet himself too, it looked like.

Immediately, Lee's eyes fell to Doby's legs, for the tight denim that would mean the calf was swelled up under there, from a rattlesnake. They liked to hang around the dry black rubber of the circle system tires at night, for the warmth.

But this wasn't a snakebite.

Lee shrugged, looked back down the joints of the circle system, instinctively checking all the tires, whether Doby had lined them all up right or not, and at first, it fit in so poorly, what was making Doby shake, he didn't even see it. And even when he did, it didn't make sense. He sorted it as best he could: because the hard freeze they usually got in January never came, all the bugs were having a heyday. Not just the ticks bunched like grapes in his dogs' ears, or the blowflies burrowing down into the dry skin of all the cattle, but the crickets too, and they usually didn't show until early May. Lately, you couldn't even drive on blacktop anymore without crunching caterpillars. It was a game to Lee. Not because they messed with the cotton much—they didn't—but because they didn't eat boll weevils, like he thought they should. Mainly what they meant was a summer thick with moths.

As a kid, he remembered, the caterpillars used to get into the school halls the last few weeks of class. The trick then was to step on them from back to front, so that all the insides would squirt out at a girl, make her squeal, run away.

It had made him smile, then.

He wasn't smiling now.

What he was looking at—what Doby was unable *not* to look at, what was making him not so much cry as just leak water from his face—was one of those russet-haired caterpillars, the kind that are fast, can hump across the road before you can get to them sometimes. The kind the animals don't mess with because the hairs are poison or taste bad or something.

This one was curled like a large, severed index finger over one of the circle system tires, drawing the heat up into its body. It was two feet long, its black head dull and rounded like a plastic mask.

Lee took an involuntary step back.

The caterpillar seemed to watch him take it. It made him feel weak in the bowels, made him wish he were standing on the hood of the tractor too.

"*What is it?*" Doby was saying, shrieking almost. Lee didn't answer, just stared at the thing.

"I tell you she left again last night?" he said, finally.

For a moment, he locked eyes with Doby.

"Her car—" Doby said.

"She walked," Lee said, cutting him short. What he was getting at was that maybe this was her—his butterfly of a wife, going backwards, to her natural state—or maybe this had eaten her. It was supposed to be a joke, some trademark Lee Graves material. When he finally got to the end of it though, he couldn't find the punch line, could just stare at the thing.

An hour later, on some internal clock, the caterpillar raised its thick head, its forefeet slashing the air as if tasting it, and then it humped over the rest of the tire, down to the ground, moving towards the professor's house, like it knew he was a consultant for the state's boll weevil eradication program. Like it knew it would be safe there, a prize specimen.

Lee hooked his mouth up into a tight smile, shook his head. "Not you too," he said, then started the tractor, got ahead of the caterpillar time and again, trying to herd it back towards the circle.

By two o'clock, throttling hard over a furrow, one of the rear axles snapped.

Beside him in the cab, Doby didn't say anything, just kept his fingertips to the side glass, all his weight there.

For long moments, the caterpillar stayed where it was, pointed right at them, but then, slowly, stiffly, as if it had bones in its body, it turned, started weaving through the stubble. Not in the direction of the circle system, but Lee's house and barn and shop.

"Well whaddya know," Lee said, shrugging, and followed it on foot.

When it got to the house, the dogs swelled up from under the shop and circled the caterpillar, their barks shrill, desperate.

Doby stepped neatly in behind Lee, keeping Lee between him and what was about to be happening, and Lee guessed he understood.

Ten minutes later, four of the dogs were dead, the fifth dying, one of the barbed russet hairs lodged in its muzzle like a porcupine quill.

Lee looked across the pasture, at the professor's white house.

"Guess I should tell her her dog's dying," he said, like he was talking to Doby. But he wasn't.

When Doby got back from the house with two beers and two sandwiches, Lee kept his eyes on the giant caterpillar and explained to Doby that, since he wasn't really working, he wasn't really getting paid this afternoon either.

Doby nodded, unable to look away from the caterpillar either, and Lee took his beer away before he could open it. Said, "Start drinking, you might want to look for another job, yeah?"

Doby didn't say anything, just went to the stock tank twice when he needed water. It was good for him, Lee told himself. The kid needed somebody to show him what was what, what wasn't.

"So she just staying over there now?" Doby said, lifting his chin to the professor's house.

Lee drained his beer, started on Doby's, and was about to say no when the caterpillar slung the front of its body up onto the concrete pad the barn was built on.

"Maybe it can weld that shank on the cultivator for me . . ." Lee said, standing, leaving his empty bottle on the toolbar behind him.

The caterpillar humped its way through the large, open door. Lee stopped at the edge of the concrete, asked Doby what caterpillars eat.

"I don't know," Doby said. "A lot. Saving up and all." Lee nodded, had been thinking exactly that same thing.

"Go see what it's doing," he said, pointing with his chin.

Doby shook his head no. "I'm not really on the clock, remember?"

Lee stared into the darkness.

There was something happening in there, something building, whirring—

Bats.

Eighty of them, maybe. They billowed like smoke through the open door and scattered in the sunlight.

"Hunh," Lee said.

"Gonna call Dave Timmons?" Doby said.

Dave Timmons was the county trapper. Used to, he'd been a park ranger over at Guadalupe. Now he was buddy-buddy with the professor.

Lee shook his head no.

"Who then?" Doby said.

"Guinness," Lee smiled, and drained the last of his second beer, slung the bottle into the tall weeds.

With dusk came Stace Collinworth, in her father's truck. Lee and Doby were still watching the barn door.

"Your ride?" Lee said.

"If I'm off," Doby said back, "or—I mean. If I'm still not on, or whatever."

Lee shrugged, said, "You gonna tell her?"

Doby looked back to the barn one last time.

"Let me say it another way," Lee said. "Do you want to finish moving to that other pivot, or you want me to get it done myself?"

"You're saying you'll let me go if she finds out?" Doby said, quieter.

"You're a dime a dozen, kid," Lee said, then turned to look at Doby, added, "She worth it, y'think? Good job like this?"

"Good?"

"Good enough."

Doby pulled his eyes away and they left it like that. He didn't even look back when he got in the truck with Stace.

One of her father's taillights went dark when the truck bounced over the cattleguard, then went red again when they were on the road into town.

Lee nodded that that was about right, and came back to the barn.

The back door had a tractor tire leaned up against it, and there weren't any windows. If the thing was coming out, it was coming out past him. Except that it wasn't.

Lee wished one of the dogs were still alive, to spell him. Alone, just to get beer and a plate of something, he had to scramble inside, bang his weak hip on the table, pull all the jars and cans off the top of the refrigerator when all he wanted was the shotgun. On the way out he grabbed the radio too, tuned into an ag show once he was sitting down again. It was out of Oklahoma. All they were talking about was the Martian moon, though, and the plume it had coughed up. Whether it was solid or liquid, ash or smoke. If it was drifting towards the sun just because everything in the solar system tended to or if it was going there because it needed the radiation, or the warmth, or something nobody even knew about.

Tumbling in space with the debris was the shattered floor of the crater the probe had touched down in. Some of the chunks were supposed to be a hundred feet across, almost, made of some kind of melted ore.

Lee wondered if any of them would land in Texas, and wasn't sure if he cared or not.

He leaned back to study the black velvet sky, the stars spinning around him it seemed, and he fell asleep like that, the shotgun across his lap, the plate of food half-eaten by his boot. It was the last of Zoe's cooking.

The next morning, the professor was standing over him. Lee closed his eyes, opened them back. The professor was still there.

"Needing a cup of sugar, doc?" Lee asked.

The professor smiled, was watching the front of the house. Lee craned around, studied it too. The front door was chocked open. Soon enough Zoe walked through it, her arms mounded with clothes from her closet.

Lee laughed to himself. "I take that back. Guess you already got the sugar, right?"

"I talked to your field hand this morning," the professor said.

"*Ex*-field hand," Lee corrected, then kept going: "No-account, no-clutch-using, good-for-nothing *ex*-field hand."

"Ex-field hand," the professor conceded.

Lee stood, caught the shotgun before it clattered to the dirt.

"He told me there was something over here I might be interested in," the professor went on, then added, "scientifically interested in, I mean."

"As opposed to . . . romantically." Lee smiled to himself, covered his mouth with his hand. "Afraid I wouldn't know what you're talking about there," he said.

The professor stared at him.

"Suppose there were a—a reward?" he said at last.

Lee tongued his lower lip out. Said, as innocently as he could, "What do you have that I could possibly want, you think?"

The professor turned away with his hands balled in his pockets.

"Anyway," Lee added. "Doby's pulling your leg, I'd guess."

"He said it got your dogs."

Lee just stared at him.

"Your dogs," the professor repeated, as if Lee wasn't hearing.

"Had to put them down yesterday," Lee said back, holding up the shotgun to show. "They got into it with a skunk or something."

"Or something," the professor repeated, lifting his chin to the open barn. "Mind if I look around for this—this skunk?"

"Be my guest," Lee told him, "might take a look at that culti-vator while you're in there," then turned back to the house, for Zoe, but saw his plate instead. It was clean and . . . something else. Past it, the last dog that had died. It had been licked hollow. There wasn't even enough left for the flies, it didn't look like.

Lee swallowed, panned across all his junk equipment and broke trucks. The caterpillar wasn't there.

"He's the same color as the sorghum, isn't he?" the professor said, suddenly behind Lee.

"Skunks eat sorghum?" Lee said.

There were worse ways to spend the morning.

He could feel the professor staring at him.

"Mr. Graves," he said. "If this—if your field hand saw what he said he saw, it's not . . . it's more important than us. Than this."

13

Lee didn't turn around to look at him. Zoe was carrying another load of clothes through the door. Her winter coats, all the way back to high school.

"More important," Lee said, not so much like he was agreeing, but just like he'd heard. Was giving it some thought.

When he caught Zoe's eye, gave her a nod, she turned away.

The shotgun was still by his leg.

2.

Doby came back three weeks later. Lee was in the field working on the broke axle, only looked back to his house when Stace Collinworth eased her father's truck along the metal side of the barn. It amplified the leaky exhaust, pushed the sound out across the field.

Lee watched Doby separate himself from the weeds and old trucks, walk out touching his lips over and over. Halfway there he lost his nerve, slouched over to the circle system to pick up where he'd left off, turning the wheels sideways.

Lee shook his head, dunked the bearing in his hand back into the bucket of diesel he'd siphoned up from the tractor.

"Guess I just told you not tell your *girl*friend, right?" he said once Doby had worked his way up the circle to the tractor.

Doby kept his eyes down, and Lee let the silence ride just long enough, then laughed, clapped Doby hard on the shoulder.

"Doesn't matter," he said. "Coyotes must have got it or something."

Doby looked up under his hair to Lee, smiled with one side of his face, and asked if it was okay if he left by seven tonight, maybe?

"What time is it now?" Lee said back, slinging a dob of grease off the end of his fingers.

"Two."

"Two . . ." Lee repeated, wiping his fingers on the pale blue shop rag from his back pocket, letting his eyes focus on the professor's house again. It was the only reason this axle was taking so long.

Doby shrugged, his eyes flaring the littlest bit before he could control them.

Lee pretended not to notice. The kid had been gone too long, though.

"That how it's going to be, then?" Lee said. "Five hours a day—whichever five you want?"

Doby pushed his hands deeper into his pockets, so that his shoulders rose to the top of a shrug, stayed there, his eyes flat and dull.

"You think you're in love, don't you?" Lee told him, trying to work a seized pair of channel locks open.

Doby raised his face to the professor's house and stared at it long enough that he didn't have to say anything.

That night, Lee kept him busy until nine-thirty.

Two weeks later, Lee backed the tractor up to the head of the circle system, feathered the clutch until Doby could slip the thick pin down through the hitch. Then, in the shade of the barn, they ate lunch, watched the tractor out there. Just figuring by distance and low gear, it would take all of twenty minutes to get the circle pulled to the other pivot. But there was always more stuff to figure in, Lee knew: one of the wheels twisting off; one of the joints getting disconnected. The axle on the tractor snapping again. Nothing was ever easy.

He chewed his ham sandwich and listened to nothing. Ever since the dogs had died—that was how he marked the day— ever since then, there had been no crickets. And if the bats had ever come back, he didn't know about it. The real test would be if there were mice living back in the seed corn or not, like there always had been.

Maybe today, if the circle system went well, he'd send the kid back there to shave off some camphor. To know if the mice were still back there or not, all Lee would have to do is keep his eye on Doby when he came back out: if he was cupping a handful of chewed bubblegum—rescued baby mice—then things were getting back to normal. If there weren't any mice, then . . . well. Maybe the people on the talk shows were right: the end of the world was here.

Lee raised his beer to his mouth and held it there.

He should be so lucky.

When he lowered his beer again, Doby was watching him.

"What?" Lee said.

"She's not coming back this time, is she?" Doby said.

Lee worked his finger up against the gumline of his molars on the right side, trying to dislodge the corner of a chip. "I not pretty enough for you?" he finally said.

Doby gestured with his half-eaten ham sandwich, and Lee smiled, understood: the days of stove cooking were over.

"I'll buy you a burger from town tomorrow, how's that?"

Doby took another bite, trying to keep his mouth far away from the ham, it seemed.

"It's quiet," he said.

Lee nodded, said, "So you ever tell anybody else? Your science teacher?"

Doby shook his head no. "What do you think it was, really?"

Lee scooped some dip into his lip, packed it down with his tongue, and said, "You've seen those—those big-ass whitetails in the magazines, right?" Lee spit, went on: "Only reason they can get all tangled and big like that, it's . . . it's just genes, feed, and privacy, pretty much. Right?"

17

Doby shrugged sure.

"That's what we saw was, I figure. Get enough caterpillars going one season, there's bound to be a freak giant or two. Just numbers. And luck. But then, what if one of them grows up or hatches or whatever under the fertilizer tank or something, right? Like down in the rack, where the seed's all gooey?"

Lee shrugged at the end, to make it all true.

For the first few nights alone, it had been all he could think about.

"Think?" he prompted, when Doby wasn't answering.

"Trophy caterpillar . . ." Doby said, standing, pulling his hat back down over his eyes. For half a second, Lee wondered if he'd ever been that young, really.

"You think it's that—that it's that *moon*, don't you?" Lee said, standing too, pitching his paper plate away.

"When it blew up or whatever," Doby said, his voice flat enough that it was like he was reciting, "there were like . . . x-rays, or gamma rays, or something. They got here almost right away, pretty much."

Lee looked up into the sky. "These the cancer rays, or the ESP rays?"

Doby was looking out at the tractor again.

"It snowed in one of those bible cities," he said.

"You been watching too much television, kid."

"It means 'fear,' that moon, or whatever. Phobos. Phobia. Stace studied it in English. If it's even a moon in the first place, I mean."

Lee eased out into the sunlight, wrapped the seed head of a green careless weed around his index and middle fingers. "What do you mean *if* it's a moon?"

"It's metal—"

"Ore."

"Whatever. They're saying nickel, mostly. Like it could be the core of some other planet, after the rest of the planet broke off or got used up or something."

"And it was filled with what? Tea?"

Lee yanked at his careless weed. It snapped right below his fingers.

"Just saying," Doby said, heading out towards the circle. Ahead of him, Lee's paper plate flattened itself into a sail against a leftover stalk of winter wheat, then flapped over, did it again, and again.

Lee trailed a line of spit down, walked out into the heat.

Three hours later, the tractor spun out in a low spot, Doby backed Lee's truck up to the front of the tractor and got out to lock the hubs, set the chain.

From the cab, Lee guided him forward until the chain was tight against the tractor, then waved for him to start pulling. Once Lee could feel it, the strain, he let the clutch out on the tractor and throttled up, and their long, ridiculous train clumped forward.

Ten minutes later, they were at the other pivot. It had been leaking like always; the ground around it was spongy and dark. Doby sprayed most of it up onto the front glass of the tractor.

Lee shook his head, swallowed his spit.

Out the side of his cab, he could see the porch of the professor's house.

Standing with one hand on one of the white rails was a woman in a dress, it looked like. Zoe.

Lee looked at her for what he knew was too long, even started to raise his hand, but then, suddenly, Doby was at the door, hammering to get in.

Lee popped the handle, turned the radio down. By the time he looked back to the professor's house, she was gone.

He cut his head back to Doby.

"What?"

"You'll want to see this."

"Pull the pin first," Lee said, then rocked the tractor back and forth until Doby could get the pin free. When he came around from behind the tire he was holding his finger, but smiling too.

"So show me already," Lee said.

Doby hooked his head forward, to the riser.

It was the plastic-looking, hollow head of the caterpillar.

It made Lee smile too.

"That all?" he said.

Doby nodded, excited. It was like an alien skull, like a roping dummy from another planet.

"Guess it did die, then," Doby said.

Lee nodded, knelt down to the thing, flipped it over. It was as smooth on the inside as the outside.

"What do you think it's worth?" he said to Doby.

Doby slapped his fist into his palm, didn't answer, just started going back and forth from foot to foot.

Lee stared at the mask, at the hollow eyes. The word he kept thinking was *carapace*, but he wasn't sure what it meant, if it was the right word or not.

He picked it up gingerly, held it up as if to look out through the eyeholes.

"Nothing," he said to Doby. "It's not worth anything."

Doby stood more still.

Lee looked over to him, hooked his head back to the barn. "Go get the disc," he told him, "the big one. We need to cut this stubble down. Lucky we didn't pop a tire on it."

For a few seconds longer, Doby stood there, sagging, then pulled himself away, to the truck.

"I'm the one who found it," he said, through the open window.

"On my land," Lee said back. "On my dime."

Doby stared straight ahead, pulled away slower than he had to, the transfer case of the truck whining.

"So," Lee said to the mask. "What do you think you're worth?"

The mask just stared back at him.

Lee nodded to himself, and, before Doby got back, baling-wired the mask to the grill of the tractor like it was a steer skull or a Christmas wreath.

Before Doby could see it, he stepped around, stopped the truck.

Doby unhitched the disc, walked the nose of it around to where he could back the tractor up to it. Lee guided him the last few feet, then connected the hydraulic lines himself.

"Where you want me to start?" Doby said, eyeing the tall grass for wherever the black head might be.

Lee looked back down along the circle. "Either end, I guess."

Doby followed where Lee was talking about, opened his mouth, and Lee cut him off by shrugging. "What? Think those wheels are going to turn themselves around on their own?"

Doby closed his eyes and Lee covered his mouth with his hand, waited for Doby to try to object. He couldn't, though.

"Stace's coming to get me at eight," he said.

"In the morning?" Lee said, then—he wasn't sure why—threw Doby a silver beer from the cab of the truck.

Doby turned it in his hand, said, "This a test?"

"You operating any heavy machinery in the next few hours?" Lee said back.

Doby shook his head no, in defeat, and Lee shrugged, climbed up into the tractor. Two hours later, the air behind him was thick with brown hawks, come to dive bomb the mice and snakes his discs dug up. As a kid himself, Lee had stood behind the tractor, throwing bottles and dirt clods at the hawks, to try to let the mice get away. It was how he knew about the handful of chewed bubblegum Doby would walk out of the camphor-smelling barn with, given the chance. How he knew that turning all the wheels of the circle back around would be good for him: because his father had done the same for him, except with an old Tri-Matic.

By eight-fifteen, Stace Collinworth's pale headlights were shining out into the field.

Lee made one more pass, then, at the far side of the field, by the fence, he cut the tractor off, left the disc in the ground. Directly in front of him, between the fence and his field, was one of the pieces of rebar the boll weevil eradication people had hammered down like a post. Balanced on top of it was a lime green lantern with translucent fiber screen—a boll weevil trap.

Every morning, the professor was out walking down the line of rebar, to do his counts.

Lee looked back to the tractor, to the black mask staring down, and wondered if Zoe ever walked with him.

Two days later they pressured up the circle system, Doby at the pivot with the power switch and the insulated gloves, Lee out at the end that moved, sighting down along all of the tires with a pair of binoculars.

It worked. None of the gaskets blew, even.

They went for lunch in town, for the burgers Lee had promised.

In the corner booth, the one with the rounded bench, was the professor. He was leaned across the table, his face close to Dave Timmons. Timmons was wearing his county jacket, the one with a bear trap patch sewn in around the Texas star, like there'd been anything even remotely like a bear in Sterling County for the last two hundred years. They both stopped speaking when Lee and Doby walked in. Lee nodded to them, touched the brim of his cap, then sat down on the other side of the diner.

They knew.

It was all Lee could do not to smile.

"What?" Doby said, his eyes intense, his fingers spread on the table.

Lee shook his head no, nothing. "Thought your girl worked here," he said, tilting his head to one of the two waitresses.

"After school," Doby said.

Lee nodded, knew that, was just killing time.

"How many hours you got coming?" he asked Doby.

"Eighty-two," Doby said without a pause.

Lee pulled his lips back as if in pain, said, "Guess you're buying, then?" but then ordered for both of them: double cheeseburger plates, black coffees.

"I don't like coffee," Doby said.

Lee studied the trucks in the parking lot, half of them with wiry-haired dogs up on the toolboxes. It was a good day.

When they made it outside again, Dave Timmons's county truck was parked alongside Lee's. The professor was in the passenger seat, his eyes hooded, intense.

"A word, Lee?" Dave said.

Lee extracted the toothpick from his mouth to study the point.

The professor was just staring at him.

"You know my field hand, right?" Lee said, stepping aside so the professor had no choice but to see Doby.

Doby nodded a thin-lipped hello, tried hard to just watch the road.

Dave Timmons rearranged his hands on the steering wheel, said, "Martin here tells me that you've maybe got something of interest out at your place."

"That right?" Lee said, leaning on the cab with his whole arm, peering in at the professor. "He didn't mention anything of interest over at *his* house, did he? Any*body*, I mean."

Dave Timmons smiled, said, "You saying the good doctor's harboring a fugitive?"

"Not real sure what he's doing to her, Dave," Lee said.

Dave Timmons craned his head around to the professor.

"It's asylum," the professor said, quietly.

"It's Zoe," Lee corrected.

Dave Timmons nodded, his eyes narrowed now with doubt.

"Didn't know this was—was personal," he said.

"It's not," Lee said, shrugging, then, to the professor. "It's *bio*logical, yeah?"

The professor's eyes heated up. "So you admit it's there?" he said, across Dave Timmons.

Lee stared at him, finally just turned and presented Doby again. "Ask him," he said. "Hate to get in the way of the flow of information and all . . ."

All the blood washed out of Doby's face.

"Go on," Lee told him. "We're all friends here."

Doby swallowed loud, touched his mouth with the side of his hand, and said, "It's dead, Mr. Blain. Mr. Timmons."

"You *know* it's dead?" the professor said, leaning halfway across the cab now, as if to push Dave Timmons to the back of the seat.

Dave Timmons guided the professor's hand away from his chest.

"Coyotes," Lee said.

"Your dogs were bigger than coyotes," the professor said.

"Doesn't mean the coyotes don't kill them too," Lee shrugged. "Right, Dave?"

Dave Timmons nodded once, like he didn't want to be involved here anymore.

"But all you found was the—the . . ." the professor started.

"Carapace?" Lee tried.

". . . head capsule," the professor corrected, slowly, like this was a trap of some kind.

"Whatever," Lee said, looking at the road now too, smiling when he saw the opening the professor had left for him: "Take *my* head capsule off, the rest of me isn't going to work so well, I don't figure." He couldn't help laughing at it, but couldn't just stand there laughing like an idiot either. He shrugged his way around to Doby, said, "Ready?"

Doby nodded, had already been eighty percent gone anyway.

"Gentlemen," Lee said in farewell, touching the brim of his cap again, and followed his hand around the curvature of Dave Timmons's thick grill guard.

The professor was waiting for him on the other side, Dave Timmons barely holding him in the truck.

"Careful now," Lee said, so just the two of them could hear.

In reply, the professor jerked his shoulder away from Dave Timmons, walked up to Lee. "They're called instars," he hissed. "Most caterpillars go through five or six of them. They're like stages."

"Like snakes?"

"Like molting, yes."

"Then where was the rest of it, doc?"

"Where was the head capsule?"

Lee just stared at him. "Tell my wife that if she—" he started, but didn't get to finish: the professor shoved him backward.

It was exactly what Lee wanted.

The fight was over before Dave Timmons could even ditch his pistol on the dash, clamber out the driver's side door.

As politely as possible, Lee let go of the front of the professor's shirt. He had been using it to pull the professor's face into the hard plastic flare around Dave Timmons's mud tire. The professor slumped into the caliche, blood spreading across his prewashed denim shirt.

"Lee—" Dave said, mustering all the authority he had, but Lee shook his head no, climbed into his truck.

The whole ride out of town, Doby didn't say anything, just sat there, tapping his fingers together in some secret order.

For the rest of the afternoon Lee had Doby repacking wheel bearings on all the cotton trailers. When it got dark, Stace Collinworth pulled up, directed her lights onto Doby, then backed up, angled her lights to the next set of wheels too. Once when Lee's back was turned, they eased the truck out, slipped away without even touching the brakes. Lee wondered what took them so long.

In the field, on the tractor, all he was doing was making one half-pass with the disc then stopping for long minutes, then making another half-pass and stopping again, the professor's house there through his windshield each time.

On the console beside him, the baling wire still looped through the eyeholes, was the mask—the head capsule.

It was hard, brittle.

Walking out to the tractor after lunch, Lee had stopped at the riser and dug all around, for whatever skin or hair the caterpillar might have sloughed off, but there was nothing, and he understood: in the dark between the two houses, the caterpillar had wriggled from the thing it used to be, and then, like a mother dog with her afterbirth, it had patiently eaten what was left over. All the soft tissue, anyway.

If the coyotes had gotten a chance to try, they'd be dead like the dogs, russet-colored hairs needled in their muzzles and mouths, their bloated bodies forming a ring around the pivot.

Lee went two full passes then stopped again, stared back at his place.

Now that Stace Collinworth was gone, it was wholly dark.

Holding the head capsule by its wire loop, he walked down the dry side of the circle system, stood between his house and barn for a long time, just listening to the air. It was so quiet it felt like a vacuum, like he was standing in the inky blackness of space, untethered from everything.

Four hours later, sitting in the cab of his truck with the radio on, he watched the professor come across the field, his flashlight ducking and bobbing.

For the next three hours, the light shone into every nook and cranny the professor could find or guess at. Maybe even the seed corn. It was mounded in the back of the old tack shed, with all the rotting saddles and bridles. At one time, the shed had been a house, according to Lee's father.

After he was done looking, the professor started looking again.

Lee could hear him breathing, and then, when he raised the mask to his own face, to look through the eyeholes, he could hear himself breathing as well.

It sounded right.

The next morning, Doby didn't show up.

Lee stood on his porch and stared across the field. The fourteen segments of the circle system glittered with dew. From half a mile away from it, and five hundred years back, it could have been a sea serpent, floundered up onto land to bury its eggs.

Except the Gulf was nine hours from Sterling City.

Zoe had asked him to take her there, once.

Lee carried the loaf of bread he was eating into the cool of the barn and studied all the I-beams overhead. If it was there, though, had spun its own silk, the professor would have seen it. Even with his eyes swelled shut.

On the way out, Lee impaled a piece of bread on the shank of an old bedchopper. It was a test. Any other day, any normal day, the barn swallows would find the bread inside of thirty minutes, pick it away crumb by crumb.

Two hours later, the bread was still there, the sun toasting it, the wind sucking the moisture out of the surface so that it formed a crust.

Lee shook his head in disgust, spit, and went to his truck for the mask, the head capsule. Just holding it made him feel better.

The show on the radio last night had been another idea about the leaky moon over Mars: because its orbit or whatever had been decaying, spiraling the moon in to the planet over thousands of years, some people were saying that that was design, that the moon had been inseminated with carbon and amino acids and RNA, so that when the moon crashed down to the surface, long after humans were gone, things could get started all over again.

What the eight-pound probe had done was open that package a little early.

Watching the professor hobble across the field, each furrow a surprise, Lee had pictured Doby and Stace Collinworth out at the old airstrip where he knew they went. They were just sitting there in her father's truck, listening to the same show, waiting for the sky to start lighting up.

Another theory about the moon was that it was Hell, like from the Bible. That all that blackness that had spewed out from it was the largest prison break the solar system had ever seen. That now humanity was going to get what it deserved, for messing with things it should have left alone.

The way Lee looked at it, if the telescopes could have all just turned away for a couple of minutes, not got any footage for the news to roll, then nobody would care about this. It would just be another space accident, too far away to matter to anybody with a real job.

Not that any of it mattered anyway.

Lee pulled the shotgun from behind the seat of his truck, closed the door hard, and went to the tack shed. In one of Zoe's tupperware cake boxes on the shelf, up by the nails, was the two-pound block of camphor he bought every year from the feed store. Lee held his face away, peeled the lid off, and chipped a corner into his hand. It made his eyes water but he held it, felt his way past all the old sewing machines and grindstones and saddle blankets to the pile of seed corn. The bags had long ago rotted away. Some of the corn had even sprouted up into the cracks of light filtering down from the ceiling. The stalks were pale green and thin, too delicate to live.

With the handle of a broken rake, Lee pushed the top layer of corn back and forth as much as he could. It moved in crusted-together plates, like continents shifting. Underneath it, a cascade of kernels that sounded like rainfall, and, underneath that, no mice, scurrying away under the floorboards.

Lee nodded that he understood, then plunged the rounded handle of the rake as far as he could into the mound of corn, fully expecting the caterpillar to sling its head up from the rain of kernels like an oversized grub, blind, snapping.

It wasn't there.

Lee tossed the camphor in anyway, all in one chunk, something he probably would have docked Doby's pay for, and then all at once, on accident, pictured Zoe again, moving across the field in her nightgown, and had to sit down.

He wondered if his grandfather, living in this tack shed when it had been a house, had ever had to watch his wife run across the same field. Maybe it was a Graves thing, repeating itself generation after generation. Lee shook his head, closed his eyes, and patted the saddle he was sitting by. It pushed a thousand motes of dust up into the slats of sunlight feeling in, and Lee remembered his father telling him that those cracks in the wall were the only reason the shed—house—hadn't blown over that time the tornado hit.

Lee had been twelve years old then, the tack shed not yet in disrepair. The question he had asked was What about Grandpa? Because the wind would have cut through the wall like razors, ripped his paper skin to flinders.

Thirty years later, Lee's father's obvious answer came to him again: he rode it out like the rabbits and the prairie dogs—underground.

The cellar.

It was the one place on the property Lee and his brothers had been told never to go, because of the way it smelled through the standpipe: like decay; like a snake den.

By the time Lee got old enough to know about white gas, how it could paralyze all the snakes, freeze them long enough to get them in burlap sacks, the rounded dome of the cellar had been grown over, equipment stacked over it, the standpipe just another piece of scrap on the ground, the wooden door one of many the tornado had left scattered across the property.

Lee stepped out of the barn, stood before where the cellar should still be.

By nightfall, it was there again, the door uncovered.

Lee watched it until a shooting star scratched a line of white across the sky, then he nodded, looked across the field at the wavering square of light he knew had to be Zoe.

What he might have said in the parking lot of the diner if the professor hadn't tackled him was to tell Zoe that, from the right angle, it was hard to tell her and Stace Collinworth apart sometimes.

The rest of the night he spent disking up the wheat stubble at last, the two fender lights of the tractor casting a sick yellow glow a few feet in front of him.

The next morning, now that it was just soft dirt again—cool, even, and moist—he waited for her to cross, to come back to him.

By lunch, he was standing at the wooden door of the cellar, his lips set.

The last thing he said to Zoe in his head was that this was all going to be her fault. The next last thing was that he was sorry.

But then he took that last part back.

3.

Two weeks later, walking back from the bathroom, Lee caught his reflection in the full length mirror on the back of the utility door, and hardly recognized himself. It was April. For some reason he had two shirts on, both faded blue, the leading edge of the two sets of cuffs grimy. The bill of his cap too. It was just about rolled into a tube over his eyes. It was the way the kids at the gin wore their caps. Lee shook his head in disgust, started unsnapping his second shirt.

In the living room, the television was humming with science. It didn't even matter if it was about that moon or not anymore. The last program had been about black holes, how you could try stepping into the swirling pit of one and it would take forever, and you'd still never get there.

It had made Lee need to pee. Behind him, the toilet was still trying to fill with water. In front of him, on the kitchen table, in a carved glass cake dish, the kind that was just a pedestal with a lid, was the latest mask, the biggest head capsule.

Lee stared it down, sucked his upper lip back between his teeth.

On top of the cellar door now was an old tractor tire. And the worn-out, three-headed bit from an oilfield drill, its teeth worn down to nubs. He'd found it two years ago, after a workover crew had finished with a pad near one of his fields. It weighed maybe a hundred and twenty pounds, looked like it could still punch down to the center of the earth if it needed to.

All that was left of the cellar door now, between the tire, the anchor, and the bent frame of an old harrows, were a few hand-sized patches of faded wood. The head capsule Lee had in the cake dish was larger than that already. And that was at least two molts ago, or instars, or whatever.

The standpipe had been easier to deal with. For it he'd just hammered a metal cap down over it, then tap-welded it in place, then come back two hours later and laid enough beads around it that you couldn't tell the cap from the pipe anymore. Not that it had been big enough to matter in the first place. But still. It kept Lee from watching it all the time. Now, when he wanted, he could just picture it down there in the dark, whipping back and forth from wall to wall. Come fall, he'd find a handful of stiff, russet-colored hairs, another black mask. If he ever even opened that door again.

Maybe that's why he'd been told never to go down there in the first place. Maybe these things came every fifty years.

Lee cradled the cake dish lid off of the mask.

It was nothing.

He shrugged out of his shirt, draped it over the back of Zoe's chair, and angled his head over to hear the next science program. It was the same comet show they'd been running every other day for a week now, the one about what comets were made of. The idea was that that's what that moon had been in the first place: methane ice or hydrogen slush or something. It was only black because it was dirty, because space was full of dust.

Lee got another beer from the refrigerator and held it to the back of his neck, stared out the window at the outline of the tack shed.

Soon enough, the mice would come back for the seed corn. That's how he would know this was over. Not by seeing them creep in all at once like a two-inch ground fog—though that he'd like to see—but by hearing them under the floorboards. And then maybe there would be another sound, one he still listened for in the morning, before he was all the way awake: Zoe, over the stove. Staring out at the tack shed too, maybe.

It was better that she was gone for a bit, Lee told himself. Safer.

Not that that thing could get out anymore.

From the tractor that first day, Doby curled around the backrest of his seat, the caterpillar had been a joke, something he could have just dragged the disc over if it hadn't been so neat to look at.

Up close, though.

It was why Lee had used five welding rods for one three-inch cap on the standpipe: because he wanted to be sure it stayed put. Because even now, two weeks after going down there, he could still hear it coming for him. The sound was a handful of dry black-eyed peas falling into water, a sound he associated with being a kid for some reason. But then he knew what the sound really was too: stiff insect hairs rustling against each other. The high-pitched clatter of twenty or so sharp feet, skittering on thin, flaky concrete.

All Lee had been able to do was turn his head halfway to the right, his chin not even far enough over to line up with the point of his shoulder.

Inches from his face but even with it, the caterpillar stopped, its own face incapable of showing any of the hunger or anger or fear or loneliness or curiosity it had to be feeling.

What Lee clearly remembered was the way his own breath had fogged on the caterpillar's plastic right cheek, and how, slowly, so as not to provoke it, he'd started to bring his fingers up to his own face, to be sure he wasn't wearing the mask, that he wasn't just seeing a reflection. But then he knew too that maybe, behind the caterpillar's mask, was a face like his, the two-day beard scraping the backside of the plastic.

He pulled his fingers into his fist, kept his fist at his sternum, and backed up the stairs one at a time, feeling each one out with the toe of his boot before giving it his weight.

The caterpillar didn't follow.

In the kitchen now, two weeks later, Lee nodded thanks to it, the caterpillar, and cracked his beer open, cut his eyes over to the sound of the toilet, finally full.

Yes, the caterpillar had let him back up the stairs, let him live.

That didn't mean he owed it anything, though.

Easter came and went in the news. The dream Lee had about it was useless, didn't even have any eggs in it.

The excuse he was using for not plowing this week was that he was waiting for Doby to come back, so he could teach him a lesson, make him do all the catch-up work. It was going to take him all summer, too. The careless weeds around the pivot of the circle system were as tall as the upside-down sprinkler heads, and all along the field, like a coat, the sunflowers were coming back, sucking every last drop of nitrogen up from the soil.

Lee watched it all from the door of the shop, his welding helmet cocked up over his head.

Inside, in the shade, he was fixing all the implements last season had tore up, and using an old stencil to spray-paint L-G on all his toolbars, and then painting all his wrenches and hammers and screwdrivers the same color blue, so they made a set, couldn't ever walk off.

35

Lying under a stripper basket, welding a screen patch over a rip, he remembered why he'd had two shirts on the other day: for the slag, arcing down his sleeves and neckline. Not because thinking of the caterpillar made him feel naked. Not because he wanted to wear the mask, to be able to hold his face perfectly still like that, give nothing away.

For lunch, he went to the diner and ate alone.

Every time he came in, Stace Collinworth took her break.

Once he thought he heard Doby in the back, washing dishes, but then it was just some other kid, a wet dish towel tied around his head like a turban.

The last Saturday in April was his and Zoe's anniversary.

At exactly ten o'clock, he called the professor's house, gave him a word problem, from biology: if it takes an inch-long caterpillar two weeks to cook into a moth, how long would it take a caterpillar four feet long?

The professor tried to answer.

Lee didn't let him. That wasn't why he was calling.

Two weeks later, May, Lee realized that he didn't care anymore if it rained or not. Usually, this time of the year he had seed in the ground, ready to push through the crusted dirt and unfold in the sun. He hadn't been on the tractor for weeks now, though, hadn't even broke back in March like he should have.

It was Zoe's fault. And the professor's. And that thing in the cellar.

Lee stood over the kitchen table again, looking down into the cake dish, and shook his head no. He couldn't wait any longer for the mice to come back. Holding the lid of the dish on both sides, he lifted it off the mask, then took the mask by the edges, set it facedown in the sink, filled its backside with water faster than it could leak through the eyeholes. When the mask didn't dissolve, he pushed down on it with his hand. It snapped into nothing, the chunks small enough now that they fit down the drain, into the garbage disposal.

"Got that right," Lee said, and flipped the light switch behind the sink. His voice was creaky from disuse.

The disposal ground the remains to sludge, pushed them down into the digestive tract of the house.

Next was the thing itself.

Lee had been thinking about this for a month now.

First he backed his truck up to the diesel trailer, pulled it alongside the hump of the cellar, walked the hose over to see if it would reach. It would. Next he walked his torch from the shop to the standpipe. It reached too, barely.

He nodded to himself, was ready, but then smiled: instead of just pulling the welding helmet down over his face, he dug through the old tack shed until he uncovered one of his old roping dummies from high school. It was a black plastic steer head with a steel post neck, for sticking in hay bales. He cut the horns off with a rotary grinder, hammered a punch through each of the eyes then wallowed them out some, held it up to his face to see if it would work.

"This how you made the other one too?" somebody said then, suddenly behind him.

Lee focused in on the black plastic and placed the voice: Dave Timmons.

"What's it matter?" he said.

Dave Timmons just stood there.

"She's not coming back, Lee," he said. "You know that, right? I talked to her."

Lee stood, wiped his forehead with the back of his arm. "This in your job description now, Dave? Marriage counseling? Or— or . . . he *wanted* you to come over, right?"

"He's making noise at the state office, if that's what you're asking."

Lee looked across the field for a long moment. "You believe him?" he finally said.

"I live here," Dave Timmons said back, angling his head over to the right to tighten the skin on the left side of his neck, so he could scratch it, "they don't."

"The boys in Austin, you mean?"

Dave Timmons just stared at Lee, his eyes flat and hard. Lee held his cap tight to his head, leaned over to spit.

"What's the torch for?" Dave Timmons asked, nodding down to it, narrowing his eyes for anything worth cutting on in the immediate area.

"Barbecue," Lee said, shrugging the question off then smiling, just saying it: "Thought I'd cook me up some caterpillar tonight."

"Lee, if you'd just—"

"He doesn't have any right to her," Lee interrupted.

"She's got her own rights."

"To come home. Or at least to run farther away."

"Listen," Dave Timmons said, trying to use his hand for emphasis, like a preacher, "this isn't any of my business. You and Zoe, him and Zoe . . . All that matters to me is that I stop getting calls from Midland."

"Thought it was Austin?"

"Austin calls Midland, Midland calls me."

"Maybe you should talk to him, then. Seems he's the one with his panties in a wad."

"He used to work for them, Lee. It'd be just a lot easier if—"

Before he could finish, Lee arced the new mask over to him. Dave Timmons caught it against his gut with one hand, spun it around to look at it.

"That enough?" Lee asked.

Dave Timmons held it in his palm like a catcher's mask.

"I can take it?" he said.

Lee shrugged, spit.

"So it's over then?" Dave Timmons asked.

"As of today," Lee said back, "yeah," and Dave Timmons seemed to like the way that sounded. He looked across the field too, then lifted his chin to the circle system.

"Prewatering?" he said.

Lee didn't answer, just waited to be alone.

This time he went ahead and pulled the welding helmet down over his face, cut the top of the standpipe off, right below his welds. It rolled smoking into the bermuda grass. Lee watched it until it quit smoking, then looked down the pipe for maybe one half of one second.

There was nothing, just darkness, and what felt like a column of heat rising from the cellar. That would be left over from the torch, though. Lee rubbed his jaw. What else could it have been, right? He tried spitting down the pipe but, because he didn't want to pass his face through that heat again, missed. His spit sizzled down the metal, stank.

Lee looked back to the shop, suddenly sure that Dave Timmons was going to walk up out of nowhere again, had maybe never even left all the way. Then Lee had to smile: Dave Timmons's county truck was over at the professor's house.

Lee pushed the welding helmet farther back on his head and forced the diesel hose down the pipe, climbed up on the tank. From there he could see Dave Timmons and the professor, circling each other. It took two hours of slow hand-pumping to get all three hundred gallons of diesel into the cellar. Three hundred dollars, Lee said to himself. It was more than he'd ever spent on an anniversary present before.

He waited until dark to strike a match, and then, holding it above the pipe, he heard a whispering that had been there all along. It was coming up the pipe but it was in the back of his head too, in the bone behind his ears, the long muscle under his jaw: Zoe. She was just breathing, and talking to herself, crying a little.

It was an echo of when she'd walked across the field to the professor's house in March.

Lee knew that should have made it easier to drop the match, but it didn't.

The first of the debris from Phobos started showing up nine days later. Just little blurry slivers of white light. On what Lee called the comedy part of the news, the Midland channel, there was a report about a frog and a horse. They were the Permian Basin Big 2 Comet Watch. According to the books, aside from salamanders, frogs and horses were the two animals most sensitive to natural disasters.

The two least likely to breed with each other too, Lee added, and changed channels, getting as far from Big 2 as he could. The horse and the frog didn't go away though, even when he turned the television off. *Sensitive to disaster*, the kid on the news had said. It made Lee think of the way his dogs had screamed at the caterpillar. The way Doby, that first day, had looked like he was going to start crying from his mouth. The way Zoe had run the night before all this started, as if the house were burning with flames only she could see. The cellar anyway.

Maybe they all knew something Lee didn't.

He took another drink, said it out loud, "Salamanders," then laughed out his nose. The reason Big 2 didn't have salamanders was because this was West Texas in the summer. The ground was baked hard like a shell. Any salamanders worth listening to had buried themselves months ago, deep. Like the shrimp.

Lee angled his head over, surprised. He hadn't thought about the shrimp in years. But—his father. That was it. His father had told him once about how, up in Martin County, just fifty miles away, there were low spots in the fields that, when water stood in them, seeped down far enough, had some kind of shrimp. They would just rise from the dirt into the collected rainwater like little aliens, pale, blind, trying to shake off the dreams they'd been locked in for the last five or ten years.

Lee wondered if people ate those shrimp, if they *could*. It pulled something dark into the back of his throat. He stepped out onto the porch to cough it all the way up, trail it over the railing. And then he stood there watching the sky, his lips still wet. There wasn't a single falling star. The only light out of place, even, was out by the tack shed. The diesel was still burning, the standpipe a candle, the mound of the cellar a cake.

Across the field, watching that candle gutter and not go out, was Zoe. She was silhouetted by the stark white clapboard of the professor's house. Like an apology, Lee told himself.

In the light of morning, she turned out to be a climbing rosebush.

Lee stared at it until a sound pulled him out to the rusted equipment on the other side of the barn.

It was Doby. He had two buckets—one to turn upside down to sit on, the other sloshing with some diesel from the tank in the shop. He was repacking wheel bearings on some of the old cotton trailers, capping them with Diet Dr. Pepper bottles cut in half. Dipping his hand into the diesel over and over to clean the races and nuts and bearings, which he kept lined up on a piece of board he'd scrounged from the floor of one of the junk trailers, it looked like.

"How many hours you got now?" Lee said.

"Counting this morning?"

"Counting this morning."

"Eighty-nine."

Lee nodded, cut his eyes away from Doby's cracked and bleeding hand. "She making you do it?" he said.

"What?"

"Come back. To work."

"Stace?"

"Got another one I don't know about?"

Doby shook his head no to both questions and Lee shrugged, rubbed his left ear loud on his shoulder.

"How long the two of you been an item now?" he said.

"Since January."

Lee covered his mouth with his hand, just smiled with his eyes, and then looked around behind him when he saw Doby falling back, off his bucket.

What he expected was—he didn't know. The professor, with a raised shovel. The caterpillar, reared up into an *S* on its hind legs. One of the dogs, stumbling back to life.

Instead it was just palm-sized flakes of silver ash.

They were drifting up from the standpipe.

Lee peeled a large piece of it off the skin of his forearm, expected it to crumble. It was like foil though, foil shot through with veins and capillaries, darker on one side than the other. Like there was an inside and an outside to it.

Doby plucked a piece from the air too, held it to his nose. "Weather balloon?" he said, shading his eyes to look up, and Lee looked with him, said it was probably just some insulation from the pump he'd been working on yesterday.

"Pump?" Doby said, turning upwind, his face drawn into a question.

"Work?" Lee said back to him, and nodded down to the hub still gutted on the piece of board.

Doby looked down to it too. Lee left him there.

For lunch—it was Saturday—Stace Collinworth took the longest break Lee'd seen her take yet.

Lee waited for her to tie her apron back on before waggling his coffee cup.

She pursed her lips and balanced the stained pot over, the toe of her shoe tapping a complicated message out on the tile floor as she poured.

"Thanks," Lee said. "Perfect."

She went to a table on the other side of the diner.

Behind her, Lee had to look out the plate glass window so nobody would see him about to smile.

In a tall ammunition box on the seat beside him, in a tupperware container packed in shop rags, was a silver flake of ash, the only one he'd been able to save. It was for the professor. Lee'd left a message for him at the boll weevil office.

Two cups of coffee later, the professor pulled up, eased the nose of his truck into the shade near the side of the building. Zoe was in the passenger seat, staring straight ahead. Lee smiled: it was like they'd come to trade hostages.

The professor ducked through the front door, slid into his side of Lee's booth.

"Nice hat," Lee said.

The professor just stared at him. The hat was from some safari costume, it looked like.

"We can't all be like you, Mr. Graves," the professor said back.

Lee took his own hat off, made a show of studying it.

"You look like you're—like you're hunting big game or something, I mean."

STEPHEN GRAHAM JONES

The professor had his hands flat on the table, fingers spread.

"If you're wanting to know if you need to spray . . ." he said, pausing to breathe in, lean back some, then shrugging as this were the obvious part: "You don't."

"Your mean your traps are empty?" Lee tried.

"I mean you haven't planted anything."

Lee didn't smile about this, just tongued his lower lip out.

"Hungry?" he said, pointing with his chin to the counter.

"Just tell me what you want."

"For what?"

"You know."

"You want me to make another . . . what was it? Head capsule? Dave leave that other one with you, I guess?"

"Listen," the professor said, hooking his arm over the back of his seat to pull himself up, his body already twisting away.

Lee set the ammunition box down on the table.

"It's dead," Lee said.

"I told you," the professor said back, studying the ammunition box. "They go through—"

"I killed it."

The professor settled back in, said, "How?"

"Fire."

"That's what you've been doing?"

Lee shrugged.

"It's in there?" the professor said, nodding down to the ammunition box.

"I think it made a cocoon, or chrysalis, whatever."

The professor closed his eyes in what Lee planned to remember as academic pain.

"I don't know why you're telling me this, Mr. Graves. Or, I—"

"It's of scientific interest," Lee interrupted, popping the

latches on the lid back, not giving the professor even the ghost of a chance to start apologizing now. "Right?" he added.

The professor stood halfway to see in the box. Lee turned it around for him like a salesman, nodded for him to go ahead.

Delicately, the professor peeled the light blue shop rags off, worked his way down to the tupperware container. With Lee's approval, he peeled the lid off, set the container down.

"*Metal*?" he said, sitting back, breathing disgust out through his nose. "You expect me to believe that this piece of . . . of *foil* came from a flesh and blood—?"

Before he could finish, Lee dumped the flake out onto the table.

It was shiny side up, sensitive to their breath.

When it started to drift and scrape towards the professor, Lee pinned it down with his index finger.

"What?" the professor said.

"This," Lee said back, and touched the flake with the head of the saltshaker he had ready in his other hand. The ash curled up around the metal.

"*Magnetic*. . . ?" the professor said, the heels of his hand at the table like he was going to push away at any moment.

"That what you call it?" Lee said back, and turned the salt-shaker upright. The ash had taken on the contours of the spout perfectly. And you could see the capillaries in it now.

The professor's mouth moved up and down, no sound.

"Can I—?" he started, reaching, but Lee slid the saltshaker to his other hand, made a fist around it.

"I'll give it to *her*," he said, tipping his head out the parking lot.

The professor leaned forward, licked his lips while he got his words right, then said it: "She's not coming back, Lee."

"I say she was?" Lee asked, his voice rising into comedy. "I just want to talk to her, doc. Pass her the salt, y'know. Wish her well."

The professor only stared at him about this, long enough that Lee shrugged, did what he'd already promised himself not do again: looked out at Zoe in the parking lot. She was still staring straight ahead, as if her hands were tied in her lap.

He came back to the professor, rolled his fingers along the side of the saltshaker.

"You can't do anything the easy way, can you?" the professor said.

"You're right," Lee said. "I'm the one who's out of line here."

The professor blew air through his nose again, but stood, clanged the bell on his way out.

Lee nodded to himself, looked down into the S-shaped hole pattern of the salt shaker for a full two seconds before realizing that the flake had even done *that*.

He raised his head to get Stace Collinworth's attention. She came with the coffee pot but Lee covered his cup with his hand, said, "Water. Please."

"Coffee's free," she said, her voice bored. "Refills."

"Just the water," Lee said back.

Stace Collinworth shrugged, followed where Lee was coming back from: in the parking lot, the professor was standing at the passenger side door of his truck, his arms flailing around in argument, Zoe just staring straight ahead.

"You do that?" Stace Collinworth said.

"Just the water," Lee said again.

She slid it onto the edge of his table thirty quiet seconds later. It didn't have any ice. Lee hadn't asked for any. The same way he hadn't asked for nobody to spit in it.

"Seen that boyfriend of yours lately?" he said without quite looking away from the water.

He wanted to touch his nose with the pad of his finger too, but she got what he was saying: where Doby had brushed the silver flake of ash to his nose looked like frostbite now. Like the patch of skin on Lee's arm. Like his fingertips. But it didn't hurt.

"Least it's not catching, right?" he said, finally angling his face up to her, his eyes roaming over her cheek and neck and left earlobe, everywhere Doby's nose could have been.

In answer, she pressed his ticket down, turned to help some invisible customer at the far counter.

Lee nodded, rubbed his nose finally, then spooned enough water onto the top of the salt shaker that the flake sloughed off.

On the way to his truck he held the ammunition box up to the professor, just showing it to him.

Behind the professor, Zoe was crying, the soles of her bare feet pressing up against the dashboard. For most of the way home, Lee was able to pretend that that was what he'd wanted all along.

4.

That night it rained hard enough that Lee couldn't see much past the tack shed. The only reason he could make out the barn was because the water was outlining it in silver. Before the electricity went out, the news was all about flash floods, drowning cattle, lightning carving up the sky. Lee stood on his porch and watched it all happen. If he had planted anything, it would be washing away right now. It was like the sky had just opened up. Like the tiny meteors the night before had scratched little tears in the bottom of some sea up there over Sterling City.

In three days, maybe four, depending on the sun, the top half-inch of all the fields would fade to white, start blowing, the sand burning anything the rain had left standing. It was why Lee kept his sandfighter right at the edge of the only field he irrigated: because sometimes you only have a handful of hours to save the whole year's work.

Unless of course you hadn't planted anything.

Lee massaged the gauze he'd wrapped around and around his forearm. The frostbite had turned into a real burn over the last few hours. Maybe because of the moisture in the air.

His blood seeped up through the clean white fiber, dried a deep red, almost black.

Lee nodded about it, accepting it too, and stared out into the rain. It was coming down at a slant, the black body of the barn like a wide opening into some other place, some other time.

Past it, through the rippling sheets of rain, there was nothing—no lights, no electricity, no dull, caged bulbs jury-wired into the breaker boxes of pumpjacks, so the pumpers didn't have to go all the way out there. It was what Sterling County had looked like a hundred years ago, Lee figured. To the boy his grandfather had been, hanging his legs over the tailgate of a covered wagon, the grama and bluestem and buffalo grass scraping the calloused soles of his bare feet.

And the sunflowers.

After a rain like this, they were going to be an unbroken yellow coat from Lee's place to the professor's. The one time that had happened before—the first season Lee'd had the circle system—all the screens of their house had gone black with the carcasses of bugs come to celebrate over the flowers, or spawn, or whatever the hell they did.

This year, though, this year the sunflowers weren't going to get that, might even die out once and for all, because there weren't any bees or moths or flying ants or hummingbirds to pollinate them. There weren't even mosquitoes out in the tall careless weeds.

Maybe a giant caterpillar was what every farm needed, Lee thought, covering his smile with his gauzed forearm. Instead of herbicide, a guard dog.

It was late.

Lee dug a candle out of Zoe's junk drawer in the kitchen, lit it off the blue flame of the stove and set it on top of the television, watched it waver and flicker and snap sparks up into the air.

He didn't know what he was going to do anymore.

* * *

Because the ditch on the other side of Lee's cattleguard was a mess, a sinkhole, Stace Collinworth dropped Doby off at the blacktop. He walked up the long muddy road touching his eyebrow over and over again, his paper bag lunch high up under his arm, his thermos swinging on its makeshift strap, boots clubs of mud he had to sling ahead of himself each step. Behind him, grinning, ears back, chest matted, was a long-legged dog.

"He was in the ditch," Doby explained when Lee just stared, his cup of coffee held close to his sternum. "Just followed me."

"More like he followed what you got in that bag," Lee said.

Doby didn't look up, just tucked his lunch high up on the tire rack, out of the sun.

"How many hours you got now?" Lee said, stepping down from the porch, slinging the grounds of his coffee into the mud.

"You don't want to know," Doby said, narrowing his eyes out at the cotton trailers. They were all done, greased and packed and reparked, ready to carry Lee's make-believe crop to the gin come December.

Lee nodded, agreed with Doby, that he didn't want to know about the hours.

The dog was sniffing around the tires of Lee's truck. It was liver colored and white, its tail uncut. When it looked up to Lee it had clear blue eyes. Lee made a pistol out of his hand, shot it twice in the head. The dog flinched away, scurried off into the equipment.

"Stace says if it's still here tonight, she'll take it."

Lee laughed through his nose, said, "That how you got in good with her? Slink around until she started feeding you?"

"You don't have to do anything to it, I mean," Doby added.

Lee shrugged one shoulder, spit. "She doesn't think much of me, does she?"

Doby didn't answer. "Want me to turn the circle off?" he said.

Lee nodded, kept nodding. "Don't take the truck out there yet," he said. "It'll leave ruts."

"You made rows, you mean?" Doby said, standing up taller, as if to see to the field better.

Lee laughed a fake, tolerant laugh. Through an old breaking plow, the dog was watching him, its face angled down like a senior citizen focusing through bifocals.

"Don't have to do anything to it," he said to himself, like a joke.

"Say what?" Doby asked, squinting against the sun.

Lee shook his head no, nothing.

The shop was dark and humid, still holding onto last night's rain. Lee stood in the center of it until he could hear his heart beating. And then he zeroed in on the phone tucked behind the air compressor. The professor picked up on the fourth ring.

Lee clamped his palm over the mouthpiece.

"This who I think it is?" the professor said.

Lee closed his eyes, lowered his hand.

"Just tell her . . . her—that her dog. It came back, I think."

The professor paused long enough that Lee could hear him looking out the window, he was pretty sure.

"You mean the one you had to shoot?" he said, finally.

"Guess I missed."

"You had a shotgun."

"I'm sure she's told you," Lee said, "sometimes I have a drink or two."

The professor swallowed a laugh. "So you want me to—" he started, but Lee flipped the switch on the compressor, drowning them both out. It cycled down six and a half minutes later, like always. Lee angled his head over to the sound that must have been going on nearly that long already: the dog, barking.

Lee knew where it was, shook his head no about it.

By the time he got to the standpipe of the cellar, Doby was there too, touching the black part of his nose with the ball joint of his thumb, like he was smelling it.

"Possum?" he said, nodding down to the cellar.

Lee shrugged.

The dog's eyes were already going bloodshot. It had long ropy strings of saliva arcing out from its mouth now.

Lee toed up a young careless weed, pushed it sideways into the ground.

The mice were never coming back. He knew that now. It was like—like Peraquat. You only used it on weeds when you didn't want anything else to grow there, ever. That's how his place was now.

"Can you shut it up?" he said to Doby about the dog, and Doby turned to him to see if he was serious. Lee was. Doby shook his head no, keeping his eyes on Lee the whole time. Lee nodded, hadn't been expecting any different answer, really.

Five minutes later he came back from the tack shed with the rope he'd used on the roping dummy in high school. It was stiff, crusted together with something. Lee broke it loose, worked the loop out until it was down to the ground, then draped it over the dog's neck on the first try.

"Wait—" Doby started.

Lee jerked the rope tight anyway, cutting the dog off.

The silence it left was strained, perfect.

Lee leaned over for a deliberate spit, then wrapped the rope once around the standpipe, backed off far enough that he could pull, snub the dog up onto the high part of the cellar. It snapped and growled, all the hair down along its spine standing at a sharp angle, its tail tucked under.

"Look familiar?" Lee said, tying the rope off on a piece of equipment.

"What's down there?" Doby said, his voice disconnected somehow.

Lee huffed out the little amusement he had left at this stage of things, said, "What you gonna name him, you think?"

"Her," Doby said, looking again at the dog.

"*It*," Lee corrected, and then focused in on the diesel tank looming behind the dog, the hose slung over the top. Past it, small against the side of the barn, was the long yellowish water tank, the one Lee used to cut the fertilizer, years he could afford to fertilize. It had a half-horsepower pump on it.

"Ready to work?" Lee asked, and looked back around to Doby.

Doby shrugged, looked to the barn too, for whatever Lee was seeing.

Three beers later—two hours, give or take—Lee was standing under the tire rack up by the house. Standing under the tire rack and watching the road.

Doby should have been back from the water station by now. Unless he'd got mired down in some ditch or washed-out low spot in the road.

Lee would have been there and back already, anyway. Twice.

If the CB in the truck was still hooked up, he could raise Doby on that, walk him through whatever mess he'd made. Tell him to just dump the water, then the trailer should pop right out of whatever hole it was in. It'd come out of his imaginary check, sure, six hundred gallons, but they didn't have all day here either. Lee wanted the thing in the cellar floating belly-up by dark, its thorax or stomach or whatever scraping the rough concrete roof.

That Doby was taking so long made it easier to reach up onto the top shelf of the tire rack anyway, come down with the lunch.

Not that it was that hard a thing in the first place.

Lee smiled, checked the field for the hundredth time that morning, for Zoe walking across to get the ammunition box, then opened the brown paper bag on the way back to the wooden chair in the shop.

It was a double-meat cheeseburger, from the diner. Lee peeled back the bun to be sure everything was there. It was. Under that, in a wedge-shaped piece of foil, a generous slice of the $1.95 pie. And some steak fries. They were soggy, but that just made the salt rise to the outside better.

"Should have been on time . . ." he half-sang to Doby, and dug in. The burger was greasy enough that there was no crunching sound to drown out the radio. Lee nodded and chewed and listened to the ag reporters talk about the rain. How the clouds last night had maybe been seeded by the dust drifting in from Phobos. That the crops this hard rain had watered were either going to be the thickest ever, or just plain dead.

Like you had to be a reporter on the radio to guess that one.

Lee curled the burger up close to the fishbelly part of his forearm, scratched his right eye with the back of his wrist, and checked the field again. It was empty. He pretended to have just been checking to be sure Doby had turned the circle all the way off, had no idea who he thought he was pretending for.

According to the national news that followed the ag report, in the parts of the world that hadn't been black with storms, there hadn't been any more meteors than there'd been the night before. By some counts, there'd even been less. The scientist who was supposed to be making the official announcement didn't have much to say about it, either. Just what Lee would have expected: that this was a once-in-a-lifetime event. And that there was still one night left, maybe. Not to give up hope yet.

Lee laughed about that, looked *over* the field this time, to the professor's house, and, when the bite in his mouth swelled past swallowing, he spit it out in a gob, dry-heaved a bit after it, then just set the burger down on the old desk he was using as a table.

He'd had some stupid months in his life, but this . . . standing guard over the charred-black chrysalis of a giant caterpillar. Telling a kid who barely had a license to pull an ornery trailer all the way back from the water station. Waiting for his wife of fifteen years to walk back across the field to him, like nothing had happened.

Lee closed his eyes, lowered his head.

The CB unit in the house that he couldn't call Doby on was the big kind that wired into the house antenna. It had a mike that sat up in a heavy little tabletop stand, like for a disc jockey. It was supposed to have been so Zoe could call him whenever she wanted.

Lee should have known better.

Above him, the sky was an unbroken, pale blue. All the tears and scratches from the nights before had been washed away. No afterimages of lightning, no heat waves, nothing. Just empty, hot; Texas.

Lee pulled his hat down lower, eased into the shop to turn the radio off. When it wouldn't—the power button was broke, had been since that only freeze, in December—Lee jerked it down from the wire it was hanging on, yanked the cord out of the wall so hard it cut across his face, then slung the whole contraption across the smooth concrete. It slid into the bottom of a stack of treated seed, punctured the bag. The seed spilled down, kept coming, looked like the colored balls of plastic Lee'd seen used for injection molding. He closed his eyes tight, set his jaw, and held onto the brim of his hat as hard as he could, until he could think again. Until a sound brought him back.

The seed had stopped spilling a good half a minute ago. This was different, less regular.

Lee stepped back and found the source: the dog. It had its forelegs up on the desk, was inhaling Doby's salty fries.

Lee let it finish, then stepped out.

The dog slunk down from the desk, gripped the ground with all four paws, ready to explode away in any direction. Its rope was all around it.

"Wasn't mine anyway," Lee told it, about the burger.

The dog just stared at him with its clear blue eyes.

"Thirsty now, right?" Lee said, shrugging to the dog. As he backed away, he kept nodding so the dog would trust him, then came back from the hose with a Ford hubcap half-full with water.

He sat it down ten feet inside the wide door of the shop, then stepped back into the shadows, his lips thin and patient.

Two halting minutes later, the dog came in, its head lowered, and Lee nodded to it. The one he'd bought Zoe back when had been the same kind, had even looked like this one for a year or two. It was supposed to have kept her company all the times he was going to have to be out on the tractor for sixteen and twenty hours at a stretch.

For a month or two, he guessed, it had been enough.

The same as the CB.

He closed his eyes, opened them.

The dog was still there, its tail swishing back and forth. Maybe two steps closer to the pan.

"It's just water," Lee said to it, his voice smiling, the index finger of his right hand pointing down along the spine of a small piece of rebar, the rebar running down the side of his leg.

Thrown right, the dog wasn't going to be thirsty anymore.

"C'mon now . . ." Lee said to it, ". . . *good* water," and, just when the dog was angling its head down to the pan, somebody leaned into a truck horn.

The dog backpedaled for traction, tried to spin, and Lee whipped the rebar hard at it. It went through the thin metal siding over the bench grinder, left a slot that bled dusty daylight.

Lee shook his head about this. One more thing he didn't need.

And the dog—

It was caught. Lee smiled: the dog had raced close enough to the edge of the door that what was left of its rope snagged in some ragged tin.

Lee let it struggle until it just laid down facing him.

"Wish you'd just stayed out there?" Lee said to it, half-smiling.

The shredded tin the frayed end of the rope was caught in had been flashing, five years ago. Back when Lee used to close the door at night, to keep the elements out. The way the flashing had worked was as a lip, lapping over the other door when they were pulled together. Like everything else, it had worked great for about three days.

Lee lowered himself to the rope to work it free, then looked up to the dog, as if for an explanation: the rope wasn't chewed through, but singed at the end. Like it had been burned.

Lee flipped it out of the tin, wrapped it twice around his wrist, and stood, studying the humped back of the cellar. On the way to find whoever was honking, he picked up Doby's lunch bag, blew into it to see what the dog had left.

All there was was a note, written on bottom in thick blue marker. *I love you*, with a heart for the love-part.

Lee crumpled the bag in his hand.

* * *

The person honking was Doby. Of course. The truck wasn't quite high-centered on the cattleguard, but the pipes were too slick for the front tires to grip on, and the back tires were up to the center caps. Behind the truck, the water trailer was sinking, its wide metal tongue gouging up a thick curl of mud.

Lee shook his head, jerked the dog forward, and started working his way across to the tractor.

This made Doby honk more, then stand out on the running board to wave with both hands.

"Like I can't already—" Lee started through his teeth, then angled his head over, to be sure what he was seeing was what he was seeing.

It wasn't Doby pressing the heel of his hand into the steering wheel anymore. It was Stace Collinworth. She was staring right at him.

Lee's mouth kept moving, but he didn't have any words. The whole time he'd been here waiting—the whole time him and the *dog* had been here waiting—Doby had been parked in front of the diner like a landowner, waiting for his girl's shift to be over.

Lee tied the dog off on the first piece of equipment he found, stepped up onto the tractor without even checking the hydraulic fluid first, and, just as he was swinging into the cab, already grubbing for the ignition, saw that Doby was still waving his arms. Not just to get Lee's attention, though. He was directing him somewhere. To look—

Lee felt his heart drop, his breath stop.

Doby was directing Lee to look out into the field. For Zoe, walking back across, the bottom of her suitcase crusted with mud.

For a moment, leaning over the wheel to see around the charred line of the exhaust stack, Lee let himself smile—at last, this was all over—but then he saw what Doby meant.

It was the circle system. When Doby'd turned it off earlier, he hadn't turned it all the way off. Trying to run without water now, the middle section had got ahead of either end, was pulling the whole, forty-thousand dollar rig out of line.

Lee fell backwards off the tractor steps, sat down in the mud, then clambered up as best he could, started pulling himself to the field, the dog barking behind him, straining against the rope.

Doby caught up with him at the pivot but Lee waved him back.

Ten seconds later, the tractor fired up. Lee fell down again, turned around in the mud long enough to see Doby jerk into the field, the big disc still hooked on, churning up earth.

Doby stopped so fast he stalled, then dove out of the cab, fell down the tire like a ragdoll, and was at the hitch.

Lee breathed in, breathed out, and shook his head no: without the disc lifted, the pin would be in a bind. Doby'd never be able to break it. A highlift *jack* wouldn't be able to break it. And you couldn't lift the disc if the hydraulics weren't pressured up. And they didn't pressure up with the tractor stalled.

There was no time to tell him all this, though.

Each sixteenth of a revolution the wheels on the circle tried to turn, a little more tension was added to the big spine of a pipe, bowing it out that much more. Soon it would crease, and then he'd have lost a joint, and the whole thing would be trashed.

Lee stood, slung one clubbed foot in front of the other, and made the overgrown pivot in forty seconds, maybe. An eighth of a revolution, for the wheels.

The careless weeds around the water were a swamp. Stepping into them, shielding his eyes with his arm, Lee was sure for a moment that there was going to be another caterpillar in here—it was the perfect place—but then it was just the riser, the patched black tube pressuring up out of it, its back arched, and the stubby telephone pole the fuse box was strapped and bolted to.

Lee stared at it, nodded, and looked one last time at the professor's house.

Like Doby this morning, he didn't have the thick gloves. And was standing in water. But he couldn't lose the circle.

With his head turned away, he pushed the switch farther down with the heel of his hand.

Nothing happened.

It was off all the way now.

Ten minutes later, the tires of the tractor spinning, Doby pulled up.

Lee waited for him to fight his way in through the careless weeds, then just said, "How many hours you say you got now?"

Doby looked from the telephone pole up to the injured circle system. The mud Lee was wiping on the thighs of his jeans.

"Twenty?" he said.

Lee laughed, looked down the crooked back of the circle. "May be," he said. "Counting this afternoon, I mean."

Doby didn't say anything.

It took them almost until dark to hook onto the circle system in a way that took the strain off the middle. Finally what they had to do was dig up the anchors on the pivot and pull it back towards Lee's house. Because hooking on in the middle was suicide. None of the struts were even close to strong enough for towing. But nothing creased, nothing kinked, nothing bent.

Lee scraped some of the mud from his face and looked back to the truck, the water tank. They were still at the cattleguard.

When he looked to Doby for Doby's evaluation of all this, Doby had to tongue his lower lip out to keep from smiling.

Lee shook his head.

Stace Collinworth was perched up under the overhang of his shop like she owned it, sitting on a metal tractor seat he'd welded onto an upturned drum. She was wearing a straw cowboy hat low down on her forehead, like a girl who raced barrels.

"Where's her truck?" Lee said.

Doby looked to the road, to town, and closed his eyes in pain.

Lee smiled, had to turn away to hide it. To the professor's house.

Through the glass he could see someone at a table.

"She watches you too, y'know?" Doby said, his voice so casual it barely even registered.

Lee listened to it again in his head, then came back around to Doby. "She what?" he said, his cheeks drawn up in disbelief.

Doby took a step back, looked to the professor's house. Shrugged. "I'm just—when we're going home. You can see her. She like . . . I don't know. Maybe it's not her—"

"*What?*"

"She stands out there." To show, Doby flung his hand at the professor's house, the front of it maybe.

Lee looked back, like anything was going to be different, and finally nodded. He didn't tell Doby what was rushing at him—how, this time of year, what Zoe liked to do most was stand at the edge of a clean cotton field. The cotton wouldn't be far enough along then to have squares; each plant would just be a red-brown stalk, four or five leaves spiraling up. What Zoe liked about it, what she said she liked to watch happen every morning, was how all those shiny leaves would be tilted over just the same, facing the same direction, waiting for day— confident that it was coming. Then, as the sun tracked across the sky, they'd move with it, keeping the flat of their leaves to the heat. By dusk—now—their heads would be nodding down, like they were trying to tuck their chins into their chests, for sleep.

The one thing Lee had never thought to use against her, even towards the end, when things were going from bad to worse, was that that sheen on the leaves in the morning was the oily residue of pesticide. That, when he drove into the field, he had to go slow to keep from running over all the poisoned burrow owls that were dying anyway.

Or, he'd thought to tell her once, to take that away as well, but she'd been in the other room, and he hadn't wanted to yell. Maybe something had been about to come on the TV.

"She—" Doby was still trying to say, and, like she could hear them—if that was even her in the professor's house—Zoe started to turn towards the window.

Lee pulled his eyes away. To the cattleguard. The water tank. The mess his farm was becoming.

"Well," he said, for Doby, and could hear the resignation in his own voice, like he was at the top of a hill, looking down on something that couldn't be beat. But still, it was easier to go down there than to keep climbing.

Beside him, Doby nodded, fitted his cap back down on his head.

It was nine before they got the trailer across the cattleguard. The trick wasn't so much a matter of pull anymore—they had the truck parked beside the cattleguard now, were using the tractor, in reverse—but how to yank the trailer up out of its hole without either pulling the tongue off, folding the front wheels under, or opening up the tank on either side of the cattleguard.

But then it was out.

"Where to?" Doby called down from the cab of the tractor, holding the door open.

Lee directed him back to the tack shed, the cellar, then used the grill guard of his truck to nudge the diesel trailer out of the way for him.

"So you're still doing it?" Doby said, standing beside Lee now. Looking at the standpipe too.

Lee nodded.

"Need me for it?" Doby said, right in step.

Stace Collinworth was rubbing the dog down now, her boots off for some reason, balanced up on a toolbar so drowning bugs wouldn't crawl into them.

If only she knew.

Lee shrugged to Doby, blew air through his nose, said, "You'll need the truck, I take it?"

"We can bring it right back."

Lee had to smile about this.

"Real fast, like this afternoon?" he said, then raised his hand to face level between them, opened it as if releasing Doby. Blowing him away.

Doby bit back a grin, his eyes suddenly shy, and Lee added, "Soon as you get that disc cleaned up, of course."

Doby kept his grin, but it was wooden now. A mask he was looking out of.

"Tonight?" he said, finally.

"What?" Lee said back. "Afraid of the dark?"

Doby pulled his top lip into his mouth and looked out to the disc, still wedged into the edge of the field. Anywhere but at her, Lee knew. She already had her boots on, even.

Lee turned away from them both.

* * *

In the house for the first time in what felt like months, Lee found that his right hand was shaking. He studied it, gave it a beer to wrap itself around. Better.

Maybe there was some way, he told himself, some way to still salvage this year. It was too late to plant, but if he could convince the Farm Bureau that he'd got something in the ground six weeks ago, then maybe they'd cut him a check. All they'd need, really, would be some empty seed bags, stamped this year, a planter that looked like it had been used, and maybe, at the turnrows, some volunteer plants where he'd stopped to refill his boxes, sloshed some seed over the side.

The plants he could get all over the county, probably. If he got them in his turnrows now, while the ground was still wet, they might even take. Never mind how many boll weevils he might be ferrying. And the seed, he'd bought it early, on credit, so that wasn't a problem. He could bury it anywhere, save the bags. And the planter would be easy: just shake the emptied bags over the boxes, so the purple dust could coat the gears and paddles.

Lee nodded to himself, stared down at nothing.

It could work.

Especially if Doby's time card was loaded, six weeks ago. With planting.

Or—

Lee let a laugh hiss out: if he could get the professor to say he'd seen Lee out on the tractor, planting. Or get Zoe to say it.

Lee covered his whole mouth with his hand, cycling hard through all the options.

He was right, though: that was the only way.

Because if he didn't get a check.

And, with a hard rain like this, the agents might just be filing their paperwork.

Lee nodded, reached down for another beer, and watched Doby through the window. He'd hooked onto the disc with the tractor, backed right up to the floodlight at the front of the shop, where the stubby little water hose was. Now Stace Collinworth was holding the water on the individual discs, Doby standing up top, stomping the cakes of mud off with his boot heel.

The third time she accidentally looped the water up onto him, he slung a handful of mud back at her.

Lee looked down into the sink, then over at the phone. Thought again of the dog's rope this afternoon, burnt through. All it could mean was that the diesel was still burning down there, smoldering like cotton, like a seam of coal.

It made sense, though: if the only air the fire could get was through the three-inch standpipe, then, once the diesel burned down low enough, the flame wouldn't lap up through the hole anymore.

What didn't make sense was there was no oily smoke coiling up from the pipe.

But there was no other explanation for the pipe still being hot.

Lee stepped out onto the porch to watch it, see if he could make out any waves of heat against the stars all rolling into place. He couldn't. And, when he looked down into his hand, there was the phone. He tracked back down the line to the screen door, then again to the phone.

He'd pulled it out here.

For a long time then, he just watched it, the phone, holding the plunger down with his thumb, and then finally he did it, what he must have meant to: dialed the professor's number.

Because he was out on the porch this time, he could watch the professor's house, imagine the phone over there, ringing.

See a shadow extract itself from the climbing rosebush, cross the porch.

A second later, she was on the phone. Zoe. Not saying anything, but Lee knew.

"You have to start it in first," he blurted out, instead of everything else he'd planned.

She didn't say anything back.

"The truck," Lee went on. "Just tap the ignition over, then give it the gas right at the end. And be sure you're not parked up against anything."

She still wasn't saying anything.

"Your dog—" he started then, the pit of his stomach falling. He didn't finish, left the phone hanging over the porch railing.

He was breathing hard, deep.

I almost lost the circle tonight, he'd meant to say.

Can you say you saw me planting?

It's not your dog.

Lee stepped off the porch as if in a trance. Beside him, the dog's forefeet rose from the ground, its nose inspecting the back of the fingers of Lee's right hand.

Halfway to the cellar he had to stop, push his forehead into the cold of the tire rack, close his eyes.

The heat of the day was still in the tires.

Lee finally leaned back from the rack, nodded to himself, his eyes narrowed on the cellar, the water tank.

At least that. At least he could get that right.

But then it took twenty minutes to even get the plug on the half-horsepower water tank motor clean, two more minutes to get it chugging.

Lee had all night though, he knew.

He climbed up on the tank to slide the hose out of its loop of wire—two things his father had taught him: never use a crescent wrench as a hammer, and never pull a hose from the middle, not if you can grab it at the mouth—was working it out when a smudge of motion wormed its way into the corner of his eye.

He was higher now, could see deeper into the field. *On*to the field.

The professor was coming across, ducking under the circle, his hand to a sprinkler to guide his head past.

Lee watched him, nodded. Stepped down with the mouth of the hose.

It was just able to reach the standpipe. It fit over it instead of in it, but whatever water leaked past would find its way to the wooden door, coat the stairs.

All that was left now was to unchock the valve.

Lee waited for the professor for that. Because maybe the thing would scream.

The professor lumbered into the floodlight of the shop two minutes later. He was breathing hard, his legs caked in mud.

By the time he made it to the water tank, the dog was at his side, his hand to the top of the dog's head, between the ears.

The dog pressed its side into him.

Lee smiled with wonder, shook his head. Said, "She's yours?"

The professor opened his mouth to answer but then saw what Lee was talking about. Pulled his hand back to himself.

"So that's where it was?" he said, about the hump of the cellar.

Lee stared at him.

"Is she—" he started, hooking his chin across the field—*Is she happy, at least?*—but then stopped.

Something else was moving out there. Someone. Her.

Lee let his eyes slide away, like he'd seen nothing.

"It's down there," he told the professor.

The professor nodded, studied the faded wood door.

"There anything I can—anything I can do to stop this?" he tried.

Lee pursed his lips out, shook his head no as if he was regretting this too.

"You do know what it is?" the professor said.

"Yeah," Lee said. "Allergic to water."

"Not designed for earth's atmosphere," the professor corrected.

Lee tried to replay this from every angle, came up empty.

"What are you saying?" he finally said.

"You ever seen rats, pouring down the side of a sinking ship?"

"Not in this county."

"But you get the idea."

Lee studied the standpipe some more. Said, "So it knows I didn't plant anything this year, that it? My farm's the ship that's about to go under?"

The professor just stared at him, opened his mouth to keep on with whatever he'd been saving up to say, but then all at once he was washed white, head to toe. Halogen white.

Doby was pulling up.

Beside him, two tires in the weeds like she wanted a flat, Stace Collinworth.

Doby left Lee's headlights on, stepped out while Stace worked her father's truck around for a fast getaway.

"Just in time," Lee announced, stealing another look out into the field.

Zoe was wearing a nightgown, it looked like. Something wispy, white, blowing behind her.

He closed his eyes, opened them on Doby, lobbing the keys across.

"Y'all see it on the news too?" Doby said, his smile so big it was infectious, almost.

"What?" Lee said, panning around, and then crouched instinctively when the lights came on above him. In the sky.

It was the meteor shower the scientists had been promising. Fire, raining down.

The professor fell back, caught himself on his fingertips, a sound working up into the back of his throat, his eyes narrowed at the sky.

It was beautiful. Not at all like anything that had ever happened before.

Lee felt down for the solidness of the trailer.

The lights were streaking now, dying out. But the tails they'd left. They were spreading, fanning out like—like all the individual dust particles were glowing on or something, arranging themselves into vast, planetwide filaments of pale yellow light, tinged with blue. And it didn't throw any shadow, either.

"Atmospheric reaction," Doby narrated.

Lee came back to earth, settled his eyes on Doby, Stace Collinworth holding onto him like he could keep her safe from this somehow.

"But—but—" the professor was saying, trying to say.

He spun around the first time the wooden door of the cellar bumped up against the rusted frame of the harrows.

He looked to Lee about it.

"It can't," Lee said, but then it did: the three-headed drill bit rolled off, the wood cracking beneath it.

"That's one big possum," Doby said, nervous laughter in his voice.

Lee opened his mouth, his eyes hot, and looked out to the field again. Zoe was almost to the sandfighter at the edge of the property now. Behind her, the galvanized silver backbone of the circle system humped up against the sky like a giant salamander, pivoting its heavy head towards Lee. Nodding once.

When Doby stepped toward the door, reaching, Lee held him back.

It didn't need their help.

Above them—Lee didn't even have to look up anymore to see—the filaments of light were scattering back into a cloud and then realigning themselves into ripples, it looked like.

Far to the east, then, what was causing the ripple: one of the big chunks of the moon was tearing down, dragging fire. It would hit Dallas, maybe. Little Rock, Jacksonville. Some empty part of I-20, a trucker pulling his wheel away like that could possibly be enough.

Lee covered his mouth with his hand, stepped back, and, for an instant he wasn't expecting but had been waiting for for two months now, locked eyes with Zoe. She was at the edge of the equipment, looking only at Lee. Whispering in his head again, only from behind, from—

Lee spun around to the splintered cellar door just as an impossible chrome moth unfolded itself wetly through the door, into the dirt.

Its skin was metal, Lee could tell, still had the vestiges of insect camouflage traced into its wings, and its eyes—blue like the edges of the yellow light had been. And alive, cataloging at a desperate speed.

The professor stood, fell back gasping.

Lee nodded, slowed to just a stare.

As if in pain then, the moth opened its wings, pushed itself over to its other side and went into a panic, and in a flash the news and the animals and the broken moon all came together for Lee, and he understood what the moth was doing: escaping. Like the professor had said. Not just the cellar, either. It was built for the cold of space. The safety of space.

The next time it flopped over, Lee fell back, took Doby with him.

The next time it flopped, it didn't make it over.

"It's dying," Doby said.

When Stace Collinworth stepped forward as if to help it, Lee held her back with his arm.

"But—" she said.

Lee pulled her away, back, back to the grill of her truck, pushed her into Doby and the two of them held onto each other, their fingers deep in each other's arms.

"It's giving up," Lee said, his whole face hot now. Zoe watching, her left fist to the hollow of her throat, that cavity between her collarbones.

"We can't just—" Doby said, trying to fight around Lee, to help this big, beautiful, dying thing, and Lee nodded, finally. Stepped out in front of him.

"Think *this* hurts?" he said to the moth, his voice rising, breaking, his hand waving around to earth, all this air, this gravity. "You're going to fucking hate this, then," he added, softer, and opened the valve on the water tank, took the hose at its base instead of its mouth.

The motor was off, had sputtered out while Lee'd been watching the sky, but the tank was still full enough that the water spouted from the hose.

Lee angled it over onto the moth's chrome skin.

The moth screamed, writhed away, and Lee stepped in closer, giving it more, more, yelling things at it he didn't even understand, and finally, just to get away, the moth finally got enough air under its great wings to beat into the sky once, twice, then higher, spiraling up towards the new light. From the pastures all around too, there were more giant moths, fluttering up into space, their skin the color of oil on water.

"God," Doby said.

Lee nodded slowly, was watching Zoe watch him, her balled hand pushed hard against her throat.

"How much gas she have in that truck?" he said to Doby, without looking around at him or Stace Collinworth.

"Quarter tank?" Doby said like a question, so Stace could nod that that was about right, her eyes hooded, lower lip bitten in.

"And mine?" Lee said, about his truck.

"I filled it like you said," Doby said, proud that he'd remembered.

Lee nodded, swallowed, could feel Zoe so close, so there.

"Take it," Lee said, and lobbed the keys back across to Doby.

"But—" Doby started.

"Your final check," Lee said.

When Doby just stood there, the keys still held against his chest where he'd caught them, Lee stepped in, pushed him back.

"Go," he said, and when Doby still wasn't, still wouldn't, Lee remembered the hose by his leg.

He hauled it up, directed it at Doby, at Stace.

A quarter tank wouldn't be enough for what was coming, not by a long shot. And a full tank probably wouldn't be either.

But still.

Stace opened the driver's side door of Lee's truck and that blue-eyed dog jumped in, took its place by the far door. Sat there as proper as anything.

"*Go*," Lee said again to Doby, his other hand at the valve now.

"Where?" Doby said, stepping back, feeling for the hood.

"With her," Lee said, his voice breaking for the first time in what felt like years, and he didn't have to look over to see Zoe cover her mouth with her hands, so she could smile.

The news reports that night all said that the world, it was ending.

They were wrong.

It was beginning again.

ACKNOWLEDGMENTS

Thanks to Boden Steiner, for this cover that breaks my heart. thanks to Nightscape, for believing Sterling City was a real place. thanks to my uncle Bruce, for having me move the circle system so many times. thanks to Brian Aldiss: your "The Saliva Tree" is what I'm so often trying to write. thanks to Kriscinda Everitt, for making me sound better than I am. thanks to another Doby, for letting me use your name. thanks to Stephen King and John Langan and Laird Barron, for showing that these middle-length storiethings can pack as much into them as a novel, if you hold your breath long enough, and dream. thanks to Samuel Delaney and Joe Ferrer, for always looking up into the dark skies, and seeing something. thanks to Joe R. Lansdale, for fleshing Texas out in the right way every time. thanks to Brian Evenson, for a precision I'm always trying for. thanks to Jeff Vandermeer, for the fastest turnaround in the industry, and for fighting the good fight page after page. thanks to my agent Kate Garrick, for all these books. and thanks to my wife Nancy, for always being there at the end of the row to give me a cold thermos, wave me back into these fields I insist on working. mostly I do it just to see you standing there every time.

ABOUT THE AUTHOR

Stephen Graham Jones is the *New York Times*–bestselling author of more than forty novels, collections, novellas, and comic books, including *The Only Good Indians* and the Indian Lake Trilogy. Jones received a National Endowment for the Arts fellowship and has won honors ranging from the Mark Twain American Voice in Literature Award to the Bram Stoker Award. Jones lives and teaches in Boulder, Colorado. Visit his website at stephengrahamjones.com.

STEPHEN GRAHAM JONES

FROM OPEN ROAD MEDIA

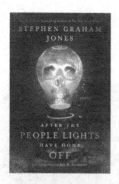

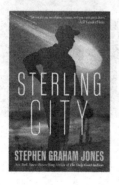

OPEN ROAD

INTEGRATED MEDIA

Find a full list of our authors and
titles at www.openroadmedia.com

FOLLOW US
@OpenRoadMedia